The Prayer

By

Violet Hunt

British Library Cataloguing-in-Publication Data
A catalogue record for this book is available from the
British Library

Violet Hunt

Isobel Violet Hunt was born on 28th September 1862 in Durham, England. Her father was the artist William Albert Hunt and her mother the translator and novelist Margaret Raine Hunt.

Hunt's family moved to London in 1865 where she grew up among the Pre-Raphaelites of the 'Rossetti Circle'. She knew John Ruskin, William Morris, and it is even rumoured that Oscar Wilde asked for her hand in marriage in Dublin in 1879.

Hunt covered several literary forms, including short stories, novels, memoirs, and biographies. Her first published work was her novel *The Maiden's Progress* (1894) which fell into the New Woman genre and represented her ideals as an active feminist. These political views led to her founding the Women Writer's Suffrage League in 1908. Feminism however, was by no means her only subject matter, with works like *Tales of the Uneasy* (1911) being a collection of supernatural fiction short stories.

Although Hunt produced many works, her reputation is as much for the literary salons she held at her home in Campden Hill as it is for her writing. She would entertain guests such as Rebecca West, Ezra Pound, Joseph Conrad, D. H. Lawrence, and other important writers of the time. She also had several famous lovers, including H. G. Wells and Ford Maddox

Ford. Ford was married but lived with Hunt at her home, South Lodge between 1910 and 1918 and collaborated with her on several works, including *The Desirable Alien* (1913). Hunt is said to have been fictionalised by Ford, becoming the scheming Florence Dowell in *The Good Soldier* (1915) and the shrewish Sylvia Tietjens in the *Parade's End* tetralogy.

Hunt died of pneumonia in her home in 1942 and her grave is in the Glades of Remembrance at Brookwood Cemetery, Surrey, England.

Chapter I

'It is but giving over of a game.
That must be lost.'--PHILASTER

'Come, Mrs Arne--come, my dear, you must not give way like this! You can't stand it--you really can't! Let Miss Kate take you away--now do!' urged the nurse, with her most motherly of intonations.

'Yes, Alice, Mrs Joyce is right. Come away--do come away--you are only making yourself ill. It is all over; you can do nothing! Oh, oh, do come away!' implored Mrs Arne's sister, shivering with excitement and nervousness.

A few moments ago Dr Graham had relinquished his hold on the pulse of Edward Arne with the hopeless movement of the eyebrows that meant--the end.

The nurse had made the little gesture of resignation that was possibly a matter of form with her. The young sister-in-law had hidden her face in her hands. The wife had screamed a scream that had turned them all hot and cold--and flung herself on the bed over her dead husband. There she lay; her cries were terrible, her sobs shook her whole body.

The three gazed at her pityingly, not knowing what to do next. The nurse, folding her hands, looked towards the doctor for directions, and the doctor drummed with his fingers on the bed-post.

The young girl timidly stroked the shoulder that heaved and writhed under her touch.

'Go away! Go away!' her sister reiterated continually, in a voice hoarse with fatigue and passion.

'Leave her alone, Miss Kate,' whispered the nurse at last; 'she will work it off best herself, perhaps.'

She turned down the lamp as if to draw a veil over the scene. Mrs Arne raised herself on her elbow, showing a face stained with tears and purple with emotion.

'What! Not gone?' she said harshly. 'Go away, Kate, go away! It is my house. I don't want you, I want no one--I want to speak to my husband. Will you go away--all of you. Give me an hour, half-an-hour--five minutes!'

She stretched out her arms imploringly to the doctor.

'Well...' said he, almost to himself.

He signed to the two women to withdraw, and followed them out into the passage. 'Go and get something to eat,' he said peremptorily, 'while you can. We shall have trouble with her presently. I'll wait in the dressing-room.'

He glanced at the twisting figure on the bed, shrugged his shoulders, and passed into the adjoining room, without, however, closing the door of communication. Sitting down in an arm-chair drawn up to the fire, he stretched himself and closed his eyes. The professional aspects of the case of Edward Arne rose up before him in all its interesting forms of complication...

It was just this professional attitude that Mrs Arne unconsciously resented both in the doctor and in the nurse. Through all their kindness she had realised and resented their scientific interest in her husband, for to them he had been no more than a curious and complicated case; and now that.the blow had fallen, she regarded them both in the light of executioners. Her one desire, expressed with all the shameless sincerity of blind and thoughtless misery, was to be free of their hateful presence and alone--alone with her dead!

She was weary of the doctor's subdued manly tones-- of the nurse's commonplace motherliness, too habitually adapted to the needs of all to be appreciated by the individual--of the childish consolation of the young sister, who had never loved, never been married, did not know what sorrow was! Their expressions of sympathy struck her like blows, the touch of their hands on her body, as they tried to raise her, stung her in every nerve.

With a sigh of relief she buried her head in the pillow, pressed her body more closely against that of her husband, and lay motionless.

Her sobs ceased.

The lamp went out with a gurgle. The fire leaped up, and died. She raised her head and stared about her helplessly, then sinking down again she put her lips to the ear of the dead man.

'Edward--dear Edward!' she whispered, 'why have you left me? Darling, why have you left me? I can't stay behind--you know I can't. I am too young to be left. It is only a year since you married me. I never thought it was only for a year. "Till death us do part"' Yes, I know that's in it, but nobody ever thinks of that! I never thought of living without you! I meant to die with you...

'No--no--I can't die--I must not--till my baby is born, You will never see it. Don't you want to see it? Don't you? Oh, Edward, speak! Say something, darling, one word--one little word!

Edward! Edward! are you there? Answer me for God's sake, answer me!

'Darling, I am so tired of waiting. Oh, think, dearest. There is so little time. They only gave me half-an-hour. In half-an-hour they will come and take you away from me--take you where I can't come to you--with all my love I can't come to you! I know the place--I saw it once. A great lonely place full of graves, and little stunted trees dripping with dirty London rain...and gas-lamps flaring all round...but quite, quite dark where the grave is . . a long grey stone just like the rest. How could you stay there?--all alone--all alone--without me?

'Do you remember, Edward, what we once said--that whichever of us died first should come back to watch over the other, in the spirit? I promised you, and you promised me. What children we were! Death is not what we thought. It comforted us to say that then.

'Now, it's nothing--nothing--worse than nothing---don't want your spirit--I can't see it--or feel it--I want you, you, your eyes that looked at me, your mouth that kissed me--'

She raised his arms and clasped them round her neck, and lay there very still, murmuring, 'Oh, hold me, hold me! Love me if you can. Am I hateful? This is me! These are your arms...

The doctor in the next room moved in his chair. The noise awoke her from her dream of contentment, and she unwound the dead arm from her neck, and, holding it up by the wrist, considered it ruefully.

'Yes, I can put it round me, but I have to hold it there. It is quite cold--it doesn't care. Ah, my dear, you don't care! You are dead. I kiss you, but you don't kiss me. Edward! Edward! Oh, for heaven's sake kiss me once. Just once!

'No, no, that won't do--that's not enough! that's nothing! worse than nothing! I want you back, you, all you...What shall I do?...I often pray...Oh, if there be a God in heaven, and if He ever answered a prayer, let Him answer mine--my only prayer. I'll never ask another--and give you back to me! As you were--as I loved you!--as I adored you! He must listen. He must!

My God, my God, he's mine--he's my husband, he's my lover--give him back to me!'

'Left alone for half-an-hour or more with the corpse! It's not right!'

The muttered expression of the nurse's revolted sense of professional decency came from the head of the staircase, where she had been waiting for the last few minutes. The doctor joined her.

'Hush, Mrs Joyce! I'll go to her now.'

The door creaked on its hinges as he gently pushed it open and went in.

'What's that? What's that?' screamed Mrs Arne. 'Doctor! Doctor! Don't touch me! Either I am dead or he is alive!'

'Do you want to kill yourself, Mrs Arne?' said Dr Graham, with calculated sternness, coming forward; 'come away!'

'Not dead! Not dead!' she murmured.

'He is dead, I assure you. Dead and cold an hour ago! Feel!' He took hold of her, as she lay face downwards, and in so doing he touched the dead man's cheek--it was not cold!

Instinctively his finger sought a pulse.

'Stop' Wait!' he cried in his intense excitement. 'My dear Mrs Arne, control yourself!'

But Mrs Arne had fainted, and fallen heavily off the bed on the other side. Her sister, hastily summoned, attended to her, while the man they had all given over for dead was, with faint gasps and sighs and reluctant moans, pulled, as it were, hustled and dragged back over the threshold of life.

Chapter II

'Why do you always wear black, Alice?' asked Esther Graham. 'You are not in mourning that I know of.'

She was Dr Graham's only daughter and Mrs Arne's only friend. She sat with Mrs Arne in the dreary drawing-room of the house in Chelsea. She had come to tea. She was the only person who ever did come to tea there.

She was brusque, kind, and blunt, and had a talent for making inappropriate remarks. Six years ago Mrs Arne had been a widow for an hour! Her husband had succumbed to an apparently modal illness, and for the space of an hour had lain dead. When suddenly and inexplicably he had revived from his trance, the shock, combined with six weeks' nursing, had nearly killed his wife. All this Esther had heard from her father. She herself had only come to know Mrs Arne after her child was born, and all the tragic circumstances of her husband's illness put aside, and it was hoped forgotten. And when her idle question received no answer from the pale absent woman who sat opposite, with listless lacklustre eyes fixed on the green and blue flames dancing in the fire, she hoped it had passed unnoticed. She waited for five minutes for Mrs Arne to resume the conversation, then her natural impatience got the better of her.

'Do say something, Alice!' she implored.

'Esther, I beg your pardon!' said Mrs Arne. 'I was thinking.'

'What were you thinking of?'

'I don't know.'

'No, of course you don't. People who sit and stare into the fire never do think, really. They only brooding and making themselves ill, and that is what you are doing. You mope, you take no interest in anything, you never go out--I am sure you have not been out of doors today?'

'No--yes--I believe not. It is so cold.'

'You are sure to feel the cold if you sit in the house all day, and sure to get ill! Just look at yourself!'

Mrs. Arne rose and looked at herself in the Italian mirror over the chimney-piece. It reflected faithfully enough her even pallor, her dark hair and eyes, the sweeping length of her eyelashes, the sharp curves of her nostrils, and the delicate arch of her eyebrows, that formed a thin sharp black line, so clear as to seem almost unnatural.

'Yes, I do look ill,' she said with conviction.

'No wonder. You choose to bury yourself alive.'

'Sometimes I do feel as if I lived in a grave. I look up at the ceiling and fancy it is my coffin-lid.

'Don't please talk like that!' expostulated Miss Graham, pointing to Mrs Arne's little girl. 'If only for Dolly's sake, I think you should not give way to such morbid fancies. It isn't good for her to see you like this always.'

'Oh, Esther,' the other exclaimed, stung into something like vivacity, 'don't reproach me! I hope I am a good mother to my child!'

'Yes, dear, you are a model mother--and model wife too. Father says the way you look after your husband is something wonderful, but don't you think for your own sake you might try to be a little gayer? You encourage these moods, don't you? What is it? Is it the house?'

She glanced around her--at the high ceiling, at the heavy damask portières, the tall cabinets of china, the dim oak panelling--it reminded her of a neglected museum. Her eye travelled into the farthest corners, where the faint filmy dusk was already gathering, lit only by the bewildering cross-lights of the glass panels of cabinet doors--to the tall narrow windows--then back again to the woman in her mourning dress, cowering by the fire. She said sharply---'You should go out more.'

'I do not like to--leave my husband.'

'Oh, I know that he is delicate and all that, but still, does he never permit you to leave him?

Does he never go out by himself?'

'Not often!'

'And you have no pets! It is very odd of you. I simply can't imagine a house without animals.'

'We did have a dog once,' answered Mrs Arne plaintively, 'but it howled so we had to give it away. It would not go near Edward...But please don't imagine that I am dull! I have my child.'

She laid her hand on the flaxen head at her knee.

Miss Graham rose, frowning.

'Ah, you are too bad!' she exclaimed. 'You are like a widow exactly, with one child, stroking its orphan head and saying, "Poor fatherless darling."'

Voices were heard outside. Miss Graham stopped talking quite suddenly, and sought her veil and gloves on the mantelpiece.

'You need not go, Esther,' said Mrs Arne. 'It is only my husband.'

'Oh, but it is getting late,' said the other, crumpling up her gloves in her muff, and shuffling her feet nervously.

'Come!' said her hostess, with a bitter smile, 'put your gloves on properly--if you must go---but it is quite early still.'

'Please don't go, Miss Graham,' put in the child.

'I must. Go and meet your papa, like a good girl.'

'I don't want to.'

'You mustn't talk like that, Dolly,' said the doctor's daughter absently, still looking towards the door. Mrs Arne rose and fastened the clasps of the big fur-cloak for her friend. The wife's white, sad, oppressed face came very close to the girl's cheerful one, as she murmured in a low voice--'You don't like my husband, Esther? I can't help noticing it. Why don't you?'

'Nonsense!' retorted the other, with the emphasis of one who is repelling an overtrue accusation. 'I do, only--'

'Only what?'

'Well, dear, it is foolish of me, of course, but I am--a little afraid of him.'

'Afraid of Edward!' said his wife slowly. 'Why should you be?'

'Well, dear--you see--I--I suppose women can't help being a little afraid of their friends' husbands--they can spoil their friendships with their wives in a moment, if they choose to disapprove of them. I really must go! Good-bye, child; give me a kiss! Don't ring, Alice. Please don't! I can open the door for myself--'

'Why should you?' said Mrs Arne. 'Edward is in the hall; I heard him speaking to Foster.'

'No; he has gone into his study. Good-bye, you apathetic creature!' She gave Mrs Arne a brief kiss and dashed out of the room. The voices outside had ceased, and she had reasonable hopes of reaching the door without being intercepted by Mrs Arne's husband. But he met her on the stairs.

Mrs Arne, listening intently from her seat by the fire, heard her exchange a few shy sentences with him, the sound of which died away as they went downstairs together. A few moments after, Edward Arne came into the room and dropped into the chair just vacated by his wife's visitor.

He crossed his legs and said nothing. Neither did she.

His nearness had the effect of making the woman look at once several years older. Where she was pale he was well-coloured; the network of little filmy wrinkles that, on a close inspection, covered her face, had no parallel on his smooth skin. He was handsome; soft, well-groomed flakes of auburn hair lay over his forehead, and his steely blue eyes shone equably, a contrast to the sombre fire of hers, and the masses of dark crinkly hair that shaded her brow. The deep lines of permanent discontent furrowed that brow as she sat with her chin propped on her hands, and her elbows resting on her knees. Neither spoke. When the hands of the clock over Mrs Arne's head pointed to seven, the white-aproned figure of the nurse appeared in the doorway, and the little girl rose and kissed her mother very tenderly.

Mrs Arne's forehead contracted. Looking uneasily at her husband, she said to the child tentatively, yet boldly, as one grasps the nettle, 'Say good night to your father!'

The child obeyed, saying 'Good night' indifferently in her father's direction.

'Kiss him!'

'No, please--please not.'

Her mother looked down on her curiously, sadly.

'You are a naughty, spoilt child!' she said, but without conviction. 'Excuse her, Edward.'

He did not seem to have heard.

'Well, if you don't care--' said his wife bitterly. 'Come, child.' She caught the little girl by the hand and left the room.

At the door she half turned and looked fixedly at her husband. It was a strange ambiguous gaze; in it passion and dislike were strangely combined. Then she shivered and closed the door softly after her.

The man in the arm-chair sat with no perceptible change of attitude, his unspeculative eyes fixed on the fire, his hands clasped idly in front of him. The pose was obviously habitual. The servant brought lights and closed the shutters, drew the curtains, and made up the fire noisily, without, however, eliciting any reproof from his master.

Edward Arne was an ideal master, as far as Foster was concerned. He kept cases of cigars, but never smoked them, although the supply had often to be renewed. He did not care what he ate or drank, although he kept as good a cellar as most gentlemen--Foster knew that. He never interfered, he counted for nothing, he gave no trouble. Foster had no intention of ever leaving such an easy place. True, his master was not cordial; he very seldom addressed him or seemed to know whether he was there, but then neither did he grumble if the fire in the study was allowed to go out, or interfere with Foster's liberty in any way. He had a better place of it than

Annette, Mrs Arne's maid, who would be called up in the middle of the night to bathe her mistress's forehead with eau-de-Cologne, or made to brush her long hair for hours together to soothe her.

Naturally enough Foster and Annette compared notes as to their respective situations, and drew unflattering parallels between this capricious wife and model husband.

Chapter III

Miss Graham was not a demonstrative woman. On her return home she somewhat startled her father, as he sat by his study table, deeply interested in his diagnosis book, by the sudden violence of her embrace.

'Why this excitement?' he asked, smiling and turning round. He was a young-looking man for his age; his thin wiry figure and clear colour belied the evidence of his hair, tinged with grey, and the tired wrinkles that gave value to the acuteness and brilliancy of the eyes they surrounded.

'I don't know!' she replied, 'only you are so nice and alive somehow. I always feel like this when I come back from seeing the Arnes.'

'Then don't go to see the Arnes.'

'I'm so fond of her, father, and she will never come here to me, as you know. Or else nothing would induce me to enter her tomb of a house, and talk to that walking funeral of a husband of hers. I managed to get away today without having to shake hands with him. I always try to avoid it. But, father, I do wish you would go and see Alice.'

'Is she ill?'

'Well, not exactly ill, I suppose, but her eyes make me quite uncomfortable, and she says such odd things! I don't know if it is you or the clergyman she wants, but she is all wrong somehow!

She never goes out except to church; she never pays a call, or has any one to call on her! Nobody ever asks the Arnes to dinner, and I'm sure I don't blame them--the sight of that man at one's table would spoil any party-- and they never entertain. She is always alone. Day after day I go in and find her sitting over the fire, with that same brooding expression. I shouldn't be surprised in the least if she were to go mad some day. Father, what is it? What is the tragedy of the house?

There is one, I am convinced. And yet, though I have been the intimate friend of that woman for years, I know no more about her than the man in the street.'

'She keeps her skeleton safe in the cupboard,' said Dr Graham. 'I respect her for that. And please don't talk nonsense about tragedies. Alice Arne is only morbid--the malady of the age.

And she is a very religious woman.'

'I wonder if she complains of her odious husband to Mr Bligh. She is always going to his services.'

'Odious?'

'Yes, odious.' Miss Graham shuddered. 'I cannot stand him! I cannot bear the touch of his cold froggy hands, and the sight of his fishy eyes! That inane smile of his simply makes me shrivel up. Father, honestly, do you like him yourself?'

'My dear, I hardly know him! It is his wife I have known ever since she was a child, and I a boy at college. Her father was my tutor. I never knew her husband till six years ago, when she called me in to attend him in a very serious illness. I suppose she never speaks of it? No? A very odd affair. For the life of me I cannot tell how he managed to recover. You needn't tell people, for it affects my reputation, but I didn't save him! Indeed I have never been able to account for it.

The man was given over for dead!'

'He might as well be dead for all the good he is,' said Esther scornfully. 'I have never heard him say more than a couple of sentences in my life.'

'Yet he was an exceedingly brilliant young man; one of the best men of his year at Oxford--a good deal run after--poor Alice was wild to marry him!'

'In love with that spiritless creature? He is like a house with someone dead in it, and all the blinds down!'

'Come, Esther, don't be morbid--not to say silly! You are very hard on the poor man! What's wrong with him?

He is the ordinary, common-place, cold-blooded specimen of humanity, a little stupid, a little selfish--people who have gone through a serious illness like that are apt to be---but on the whole, a good husband, a good father, a good citizen--'

'Yes, and his wife is afraid of him, and his child hates him!' exclaimed Esther.

'Nonsense!' said Dr Graham sharply. 'The child is spoilt. Only children are apt to be--and the mother wants a change or a tonic of some kind. I'll go and talk to her when I have time. Go along and dress. Have you forgotten that George Graham is coming to dinner?'

After she had gone the doctor made a note on the corner of his blotting-pad, 'Mem.: to go and see Mrs Arne,' and dismissed the subject of the memorandum entirely from his mind.

George Graham was the doctor's nephew, a tall, weedy, cumbrous young man, full of fads and fallacies, with a gentle manner that somehow inspired confidence. He was several years younger than Esther, who loved to listen to his semi-scientific, semi-romantic stories of things met with in the course of his profession. 'Oh, I come across very queer things!' he would say mysteriously.

'There's a queer little widow--!'

'Tell me about your little widow?' asked Esther that day after dinner, when, her father having gone back to his study, she and her cousin sat together as usual.

He laughed.

'You like to hear of my professional experiences? Well, she certainly interested me,' he said thoughtfully. 'She is an odd psychological study in her way. I wish I could come across her again.'

'Where did you come across her, and what is her name?'

'I don't know her name, I don't want to; she is not a personage to me, only a case. I hardly know her face even. I have never seen it except in the twilight. But I gathered that she lived somewhere in Chelsea, for she came out on to the Embankment with only a kind of lacy thing over her head; she can't live far off, I fancy.'

Esther became instantly attentive. 'Go on,' she said.

'It was three weeks ago,' said George Graham. 'I was coming along the Embankment about ten o'clock. I walked through that little grove, you know, just between Cheyne Walk and the river, and I heard in there someone sobbing very bitterly. I looked and saw a woman sitting on a seat, with her head in her hands, crying. I was most awfully sorry, of course, and I thought I could perhaps do something for her, get her a glass of water, or salts, or something. I took her for a woman of the people--it was quite dark, you know. So I asked her very politely if I could do anything for her, and then I noticed her hands--they were quite white and covered with diamonds.'

'You were sorry you spoke, I suppose,' said Esther.

'She raised her head and said--I believe she laughed--"Are you going to tell me to move on?"'

'She thought you were a policeman?'

'Probably--if she thought at all--but she was in a semi-dazed condition. I told her to wait till I came back, and dashed round the corner to the chemist's and bought a bottle of salts. She thanked me, and made a little effort to rise and go away. She seemed very weak. I told her I was a medical man, I started in and talked to her.'

'And she to you?'

'Yes, quite straight. Don't you know that women always treat a doctor as if he were one step removed from their father confessor--not human--not in the same category as themselves? It is not complimentary to one as a man, but one hears a good deal one would not otherwise hear. She ended by telling me all about herself--in a veiled way, of course. It soothed her--relieved her---she seemed not to have had an outlet for years!'

'To a mere stranger!'

'To a doctor. And she did not know what she was saying half the time. She was hysterical, of course. Heavens! what nonsense she talked! She spoke of herself as a person somehow haunted, cursed by some malign fate, a victim of some fearful spiritual catastrophe, don't you know? I let her run on. She was convinced of the reality of a sort of "doom" that she had fancied had befallen her. It was quite pathetic. Then it got rather chilly--she shivered--I suggested her going in. She shrank back; she said, "If you only knew what a relief it is, how much less miserable I am out here! I can breathe; I can live--it is my only glimpse of the world that is alive--I live in a grave--oh, let me stay!" She seemed positively afraid to go home.

'Perhaps someone bullied her at home.'

'I suppose so, but then--she had no husband. He died, she told me, years ago. She had adored him, she said--'

'Is she pretty?'

'Pretty! Well, I hardly noticed. Let me see! Oh, yes, I suppose she was pretty--no, now I think of it, she would be too worn and faded to be what you call pretty.'

Esther smiled.

'Well, we sat there together for quite an hour, then the clock of Chelsea church struck eleven, and she got up and said "Good-bye," holding out her hand quite naturally, as if our meeting and conversation had been nothing out of the common. There was a sound like a dead leaf trailing across the walk and she was gone.

'Didn't you ask if you should see her again?'

'That would have been a mean advantage to take.'

'You might have offered to see her home.'

'I saw she did not mean me to.'

'She was a lady, you say,' pondered Esther. 'How was she dressed?'

'Oh, all right, like a lady--in black--mourning, I suppose. She has dark crinkly hair, and her eyebrows are very thin and arched--I noticed that in the dusk.'

'Does this photograph remind you of her?' asked Esther suddenly, taking him to the mantelpiece.

'Rather!'

'Alice! Oh, it couldn't be--she is not a widow, her husband is alive--has your friend any children?'

'Yes, one, she mentioned it.'

'How old?'

'Six years old, I think she said. She talks of the "responsibility of bringing up an orphan".'

'George, what time is it?' Esther asked suddenly.

'About nine o'clock.'

'Would you mind coming out with me?'

'I should like it. Where shall we go?'

'To St Adhelm's! It is close by here. There is a special late service tonight, and Mrs Arne is sure to be there.'

'Oh, Esther--curiosity!'

'No, not mere curiosity. Don't you see if it is my Mrs Arne who talked to you like this, it is very serious? I have thought her ill for a long time; but as ill as that--'

At St Adhelm's Church, Esther Graham pointed out a woman who was kneeling beside a pillar in an attitude of intense devotion and abandonment. She rose from her knees, and turned her rapt face up towards the pulpit whence the Reverend Ralph Bligh was holding his impassioned discourse. George Graham touched his cousin on the shoulder, and motioned to her to leave her place on the outermost rank of worshippers.

'That is the woman!' said he.

Chapter IV

'Mem.: to go and see Mrs Arne.' The doctor came across this note in his blotting-pad one day six weeks later. His daughter was out of town. He had heard nothing of the Arnes since her departure. He had promised to go and see her. He was a little conscience-stricken. Yet another week elapsed before he found time to call upon the daughter of his old tutor.

At the corner of Tite Street he met Mrs Arne's husband, and stopped. A doctor's professional kindliness of manner is, or ought to be, independent of his personal likings and dislikings, and there was a pleasant cordiality about his greeting which should have provoked a corresponding fervour on the part of Edward Arne.

'How are you, Arne?' Graham said. 'I was on my way to call on your wife.'

'Ah--yes!' said Edward Arne, with the ascending inflection of polite acquiescence. A ray of blue from his eyes rested transitorily on the doctor's face, and in that short moment the latter noted its intolerable vacuity, and for the first time in his life he felt a sharp pang of sympathy for the wife of such a husband.

'I suppose you are off to your club?--er--good bye!' he wound up abruptly. With the best will in the world he somehow found it almost impossible to carry on a conversation with Edward Arne, who raised his hand to his hat-brim in token of salutation, smiled sweetly, and walked on.

'He really is extraordinarily good-looking,' reflected the doctor, as he watched him down the street and safely over the crossing with a certain degree of solicitude for which he could not exactly account. 'And yet one feels one's vitality ebbing out at the finger-ends as one talks to him. I shall begin to believe in Esther's absurd fancies about him soon. Ah, there's the little girl!'.he exclaimed, as he turned into Cheyne Walk and caught sight of her with her nurse, making violent demonstrations to attract his attention. 'She is alive, at any rate. How is your mother, Dolly?' he asked.

'Quite well, thank you,' was the child's reply. She added, 'She's crying. She sent me away because I looked at her. So I did. Her cheeks are quite red.'

'Run away--run away and play!' said the doctor nervously. He ascended the steps of the house, and rang the bell very gently and neatly.

'Not at--' began Foster, with the intonation of polite falsehood, but stopped on seeing the doctor, who, with his daughter, was a privileged person. 'Mrs Arne will see you, Sir.'

'Mrs Arne is not alone?' he said interrogatively.

'Yes, Sir, quite alone. I have just taken tea in.'

Dr Graham's doubts were prompted by the low murmur as of a voice, or voices, which came to him through the open door of the room at the head of the stairs. He paused and listened while Foster stood by, merely remarking, 'Mrs Arne do talk to herself sometimes, Sir.'

It was Mrs Arne's voice--the doctor recognised it now. It was not the voice of a sane or healthy woman. He at once mentally removed his visit from the category of a morning call, and prepared for a semi-professional inquiry.

'Don't announce me,' he said to Foster, and quietly entered the back drawing-room, which was separated by a heavy tapestry portière from the room where Mrs Arne sat, with an open book on the table before her, from which she had been apparently reading aloud. Her hands were now clasped tightly over her face, and when, presently, she removed them and began feverishly to turn page after page of her book, the crimson of her cheeks was seamed with white where her fingers had impressed themselves.

The doctor wondered if she saw him, for though her eyes were fixed in his direction, there was no apprehension in them. She went on reading, and it was the text, mingled with passionate interjection and fragmentary utterances, of the Burial Service that met his ears.

'"For as in Adam all die!" All die! It says all! For he must reign...The last enemy that shall be destroyed is Death. What shall they do if the dead rise not at all!...I die daily...! Daily!

No, no, better get it over...dead and buried...out of sight, out of mind...under a stone. Dead men don't come back...Go on! Get it over. I want to hear the earth rattle on the coffin, and then I shall know it is done. "Flesh and blood cannot inherit!" Oh, what did I do? What have I done? Why did I wish it so fervently? Why did I pray for it so earnestly? God gave me my wish--'

'Alice! Alice!' groaned the doctor.

She looked up. '"When this corruptible shall have put on incorruption--" "Dust to dust, ashes to ashes, earth to earth--" Yes, that is it. "After death, though worms destroy this body--"'

She flung the book aside and sobbed.

'That is what I was afraid of. My God! My God! Down there--in the dark--for ever and ever and ever! I could not bear to think of it! My Edward! And so I interfered . . and prayed . . and prayed till...Oh! I am punished. Flesh and blood could not inherit! I kept him there--I would not let him go . . I kept him...I prayed . . I denied him Christian burial...Oh, how could I know.

'Good heavens, Alice!' said Graham, coming sensibly forward, 'what does this mean? I have heard of schoolgirls going through the marriage service by themselves, but the burial service--'

He laid down his hat and went on severely, 'What have you to do with such things? Your child is flourishing--your husband alive and here--'

'And who kept him here?' interrupted Alice Arne fiercely, accepting the fact of his appearance without comment.

'You did,' he answered quickly, 'with your care and tenderness. I believe the warmth of your body, as you lay beside him for that half-hour, maintained the vital heat during that extraordinary suspension of the heart's action, which made us all give him up for dead. You were his best doctor, and brought him back to us.'

'Yes, it was I--it was I--you need not tell me it was I!'

'Come, be thankful!' he said cheerfully. 'Put that book away, and give me some tea, I'm very cold.'

'Oh, Dr Graham, how thoughtless of me!' said Mrs Arne, rallying at the slight imputation on her politeness he had purposely made. She tottered to the bell and rang it before he could anticipate her.

'Another cup,' she said quite calmly to Foster, who answered it. Then she sat down quivering all over with the suddenness of the constraint put upon her.

'Yes, sit down and tell me all about it,' said Dr Graham goodhumouredly, at the same time observing her with the closeness he gave to difficult cases.

'There is nothing to tell,' she said simply, shaking her head, and futilely altering the position of the tea-cups on the tray. 'It all happened years ago. Nothing can be done now. Will you have sugar?'

He drank his tea and made conversation. He talked to her of some Dante lectures she was attending; of some details connected with her child's Kindergarten classes. These subjects did not interest her. There was a subject she wished to discuss, he could see that a question trembled on her tongue, and tried to lead up to it.

She introduced it herself, quite quietly, over a second cup. 'Sugar, Dr Graham? I forget. Dr Graham, tell me, do you believe that prayers--wicked unreasonable prayers--are granted?'

He helped himself to another slice of bread and butter before answering.

'Well,' he said slowly, 'it seems hard to believe that every fool who has a voice to pray with, and a brain where to conceive idiotic requests with, should be permitted to interfere with the economy of the universe. As a rule, if people were long-sighted enough to see the result of their petitions, I fancy very few of us would venture to interfere.'

Mrs Arne groaned.

She was a good Churchwoman, Graham knew, and he did not wish to sap her faith in any way, so he said no more, but inwardly wondered if a too rigid interpretation of some of the religious dogmas of the Vicar of St Adhelm's, her spiritual adviser, was not the clue to her distress. Then she put another question---'Eh! What?' he said. 'Do I believe in ghosts? I will believe you if you will tell me you have seen one.

'You know, Doctor,' she went on, 'I was always afraid of ghosts--of spirits--things unseen. I couldn't ever read about them. I could not bear the idea of some one in the room with me that I could not see. There was a text that always frightened me that hung up in my room: "Thou, God, seest me!" It frightened me when I was a child, whether I had been doing wrong or not. But now,' shuddering, 'I think there are worse things than ghosts.'

'Well, now, what sort of things?' he asked good-humouredly. 'Astral bodies--?'

She leaned forward and laid her hot hand on his.

'Oh, Doctor, tell me, if a spirit--without the body we know it by--is terrible, what of a body'--her voice sank to a whisper, 'a body--senseless--lonely--stranded on this earth---without a spirit?'

She was watching his face anxiously. He was divided between a morbid inclination to laugh and the feeling of intense discomfort provoked by this wretched scene. He longed to give the conversation a more cheerful turn, yet did not wish to offend her by changing it too abruptly.

'I have heard of people not being able to keep body and soul together,' he replied at last, 'but I am not aware that practically such a division of forces has ever been achieved. And if we could only accept the theory of the de-spiritualised body, what a number of antipathetic people now wandering about in the world it would account for!'

The piteous gaze of her eyes seemed to seek to ward off the blow of his misplaced jocularity.

He left his seat and sat down on the couch beside her.

'Poor child! poor girl! you are ill, you are over-excited. What is it? Tell me,' he asked her as tenderly as the father she had lost in early life might have done. Her head sank on his shoulder.

'Are you unhappy?' he asked her gently.

'Yes!'

'You are too much alone. Get your mother or your sister to come and stay with you.'

'They won't come,' she wailed. 'They say the house is like a grave. Edward has made himself a study in the basement. It's an impossible room--but he has moved all his things in, and I can't--I won't go to him there...'

'You're wrong. For it's only a fad,' said Graham, 'he'll tire of it. And you must see more people somehow. It's a pity my daughter is away. Had you any visitors today?'

'Not a soul has crossed the threshold for eighteen days.'

'We must change all that,' said the doctor vaguely. 'Meantime you must cheer up. Why, you have no need to think of ghosts and graves--no need to be melancholy--you have your husband and your child--'

'I have my child--yes.'

The doctor took hold of Mrs Arne by the shoulder and held her a little away from him. He thought he had found the cause of her trouble--a more commonplace one than he had supposed.

'I have known you, Alice, since you were a child,' he said gravely. 'Answer me! You love your husband, don't you?'

'Yes.' It was as if she were answering futile prefatory questions in the witness-box. Yet he saw by the intense excitement in her eyes that he had come to the point she feared, and yet desired to bring forward.

'And he loves you?'

She was silent.

'Well, then, if you love each other, what more can you want? Why do you say you have only your child in that absurd way?'

She was still silent, and he gave her a little shake.

'Tell me, have you and he had any difference lately? Is there any--coldness--any--temporary estrangement between you?'

He was hardly prepared for the burst of foolish laughter that proceeded from the demure Mrs Arne as she rose and confronted him, all the blood in her body seeming for the moment to rush to her usually pale cheeks.

'Coldness! Temporary estrangement! If that were all' Oh, is every one blind but me? There is all the world

between us!--all the difference between this world and
the next!'.She sat down again beside the doctor and
whispered in his ear, and her words were like a breath of
hot wind from some Gehenna of the soul.

'Oh, Doctor, I have borne it for six years, and I must
speak. No other woman could bear what I have borne,
and yet be alive! And I loved him so; you don't know
how I loved him! That was it--that was my crime--'

'Crime?' repeated the doctor.

'Yes, crime! It was impious, don't you see? But I have
been punished. Oh, Doctor, you don't know what my
life is! Listen! Listen! I must tell you. To live with a--At
first before I guessed when I used to put my arms round
him, and he merely submitted--and then it dawned on
me what I was kissing! It is enough to turn a living
woman into stone--for I am living, though sometimes I
forget it. Yes, I am a live woman, though I live in a grave.
Think what it is!--to wonder every night if you will be
alive in the morning, to lie down every night in an open
grave--to smell death in every corner--every room--to
breathe death--to touch it...'

The portière in front of the door shook, a hoopstick
parted it, a round white clad bundle supported on a pair
of mottled red legs peeped in, pushing a hoop in front of
her. The child made no noise. Mrs Arne seemed to have
heard her, however. She slewed round violently as she sat

on the sofa beside Dr Graham, leaving her hot hands clasped in his.

'You ask Dolly,' she exclaimed. 'She knows it, too-- she feels it.'

'No, no, Alice, this won't do!' the doctor adjured her very low. Then he raised his voice and ordered the child from the room. He had managed to lift Mrs Arne's feet and laid her full length on the sofa by the time the maid reappeared. She had fainted.

He pulled down her eyelids and satisfied himself as to certain facts he had up till now dimly apprehended. When Mrs Arne's maid returned, he gave her mistress over to her care and proceeded to Edward Arne's new study in the basement.

'Morphia!' he muttered to himself, as he stumbled and faltered through gaslit passages, where furtive servants eyed him and scuttled to their burrows.

'What is he burying himself down here for?' he thought. 'Is it to get out of her way? They are a nervous pair of them!'

Arne was sunk in a large arm-chair drawn up before the fire. There was no other light, except a faint reflection from the gas-lamp in the road, striking down past the iron bars of the window that was sunk below the level of the street. The room was comfortless and empty, there was little furniture in it except a large bookcase at Arne's right hand and a table with a Tantalus on it standing some way off. There was a faded portrait in pastel of Alice Arne over the mantelpiece, and beside it, a poor pendant, a pen and ink sketch of the master of the house. They were quite discrepant, in size and medium, but they appeared to look at each other with the stolid attentiveness of newly married people.

'Seedy, Arne?' Graham said.

'Rather, today. Poke the fire for me, will you?'

'I've known you quite seven years,' said the doctor cheerfully, 'so I presume I can do that...

There, now!...And I'll presume further--What have we got here?'

He took a small bottle smartly out of Edward Arne's fingers and raised his eyebrows. Edward Arne had rendered it up agreeably; he did not seem upset or annoyed.

'Morphia. It isn't a habit. I only got hold of the stuff yesterday--found it about the house.

Alice was very jumpy all day, and communicated her nerves to me, I suppose. I've none as a rule, but do you know, Graham, I seem to be getting them--feel things a good deal more than I did, and want to talk about them.'

'What, are you growing a soul?' said the doctor carelessly, lighting a cigarette.

'Heaven forbid!' Arne answered equably. 'I've done very well without it all these years. But I'm fond of old Alice, you know, in my own way. When I was a young man, I was quite different. I took things hardly and got excited about them. Yes, excited. I was wild about Alice, wild! Yes, by Jove! though she has forgotten all about it.'

'Not that, but still it's natural she should long for some little demonstration of affection now and then...and she'd be awfully distressed if she saw you fooling with a bottle of morphia!

You know, Arne, after that narrow squeak you had of it six years ago, Alice and I have a good right to consider that your life belongs to us!'

Edward Arne settled in his chair and replied, rather fretfully---'All very well, but you didn't manage to do the job thoroughly. You didn't turn me out lively enough to please Alice. She's annoyed because when I take her in my arms, I don't hold her tight enough. I'm too quiet, too languid!...Hang it all, Graham, I believe she'd like me to stand for Parliament!...Why can't she let me just go along my own way? Surely a man who's come through an illness like mine can be let off parlour tricks? All this worry--it culminated the other day when I said I wanted to colonise a room down here, and did, with a spurt that took it out of me horribly,--all this worry, I say, seeing her upset and so on, keeps me low, and so I feel as if I wanted to take drugs to soothe me.'

'Soothe!' said Graham. 'This stuff is more than soothing if you take enough of it. I'll send you something more like what you want, and I'll take this away, by your leave.'

'I really can't argue!' replied Arne...'If you see Alice, tell her you find me fairly comfortable and don't put her off this room. I really like it best. She can come and see me here, I keep a good fire, tell her...I feel as if I wanted to sleep. . .' he added brusquely.

You have been indulging already,' said Graham softly. Arne had begun to doze off. His cushion had sagged down, the doctor stooped to rearrange it, carelessly laying the little phial for the moment in a crease of the rug covering the man's knees.

Mrs Arne in her mourning dress was crossing the hall as he came to the top of the basement steps and pushed open the swing door. She was giving some orders to Foster, the butler, who disappeared as the doctor advanced.

'You're about again,' he said, 'good girl!'

'Too silly of me,' she said, 'to be hysterical! After all these years! One should be able to keep one's own counsel. But it is over now, I promise I will never speak of it again.'

'We frightened poor Dolly dreadfully. I had to order her out like a regiment of soldiers.'

'Yes, I know. I'm going to her now.'

On his suggestion that she should look in on her husband first she looked askance.

'Down there!'

'Yes, that's his fancy. Let him be. He is a good deal depressed about himself and you. He notices a great deal more than you think. He isn't quite as apathetic as you describe him to be...

Come here!' He led her into the unlit dining-room a little way. 'You expect too much, my dear.

You do really! You make too many demands on the vitality you saved.'

'What did one save him for?' she asked fiercely. She continued more quietly, 'I know. I am going to be different.'

'Not you,' said Graham fondly. He was very partial to Alice Arne in spite of her silliness.

'You'll worry about Edward till the end of the chapter. I know you. And'--he turned her round by the shoulder so that she fronted the light in the hall--'you elusive thing, let me have a good look at you...Hum! Your eyes, they're a bit starey...'

He let her go again with a sigh of impotence. Something must be done...soon...he must think...He got hold of his coat and began to get into it Mrs Arne smiled, buttoned a button for him and then opened the front door, like a good hostess, a very little way. With a quick flirt of his hat he was gone, and she heard the clap of his brougham door and the order 'Home'.

'Been saying good-bye to that thief Graham?' said her husband gently, when she entered his room, her pale eyes staring a little, her thin hand busy at the front of her dress.

'Thief? Why? One moment! Where's your switch?'

She found it and turned on a blaze of light from which her husband seemed to shrink.

'Well, he carried off my drops. Afraid of my poisoning myself, I suppose?'

'Or acquiring the morphia habit,' said his wife in a dull level voice, 'as I have.'

She paused. He made no comment. Then, picking up the little phial Dr Graham had left in the crease of the rug, she spoke---'You are the thief, Edward, as it happens, this is mine.'

'Is it? I found it knocking about: I didn't know it was yours. Well, will you give me some?'

'I will, if you like.'

'Well, dear, decide. You know I am in your hands and Graham's. He was rubbing that into me today.'

'Poor lamb!' she said derisively; 'I'd not allow my doctor, or my wife either, to dictate to me whether I should put an end to myself, or not.'

'Ah, but you've got a spirit, you see!' Arne yawned. 'However, let me have a go at the stuff and then you put it on top of the wardrobe or a shelf, where I shall know it is, but never reach out to get it, I promise you.'

'No, you wouldn't reach out a hand to keep yourself alive, let alone kill yourself,' said she.

'That is you all over, Edward.'

'And don't you see that is why I did die,' he said, with earnestness unexpected by her. 'And then, unfortunately, you and Graham bustled up and wouldn't

let Nature take its course...I rather wish you hadn't been
so officious.'

'And let you stay dead,' said she carelessly. 'But at
the time I cared for you so much that I should have had
to kill myself, or commit suttee like a Bengali widow. Ah,
well!'

She reached out for a glass half-full of water that
stood on the low ledge of a bookcase close by the arm of
his chair...'Will this glass do? What's in it? Only water?
How much morphia shall I give you? An overdose?'

'I don't care if you do, and that's a fact.'

'It was a joke, Edward,' she said piteously.

'No joke to me. This fag end of life I've clawed hold
of, doesn't interest me. And I'm bound to be interested
in what I'm doing or I'm no good. I'm no earthly good
now. I don't enjoy life, I've nothing to enjoy it with--in
here--' he struck his breast. 'It's like a dull party one goes
to by accident. All I want to do is to get into a cab and
go home.'

His wife stood over him with the half-full glass in
one hand and the little bottle in the other.

Her eyes dilated...her chest heaved.

'Edward!' she breathed. 'Was it all so useless?'

'Was what useless? Yes, as I was telling you, I go as one in a dream--a bad, bad dream, like the dreams I used to have when I overworked at college. I was brilliant, Alice, brilliant, do you hear? At some cost, I expect! Now I hate people--my fellow creatures. I've left them. They come and go, jostling me, and pushing me, on the pavements as I go along, avoiding them. Do you know where they should be, really, in relation to me?'

He rose a little in his seat--she stepped nervously aside, made as if to put down the bottle and the glass she was holding, then thought better of it and continued to extend them mechanically.

'They should be over my head. I've already left them and their petty nonsense of living. They mean nothing to me, no more than if they were ghosts walking. Or perhaps, it's I who am a ghost to them?...You don't understand it. It's because I suppose you have no imagination. You just know what you want and do your best to get it. You blurt out your blessed petition to your Deity and the idea that you're irrelevant never enters your head, soft, persistent, High Church thing that you are!...'

Alice Arne smiled, and balanced the objects she was holding. He motioned her to pour out the liquid from one to the other, but she took no heed; she was listening with all her ears. It was the nearest approach to the language of compliment, to anything in the way of loverlike personalities that she had heard fall from his lips since his illness. He went on, becoming as it were lukewarm to his subject---'But the worst of it is that once break the cord that links you to humanity--it can't be mended.

Man doesn't live by bread alone...or lives to disappoint you. What am I to you, without my own poor personality?...Don't stare so, Alice! I haven't talked so much or so intimately for ages, have I? Let me try and have it out...Are you in any sort of hurry?'

'No, Edward.'

'Pour that stuff out and have done...Well, Alice, it's a queer feeling, I tell you. One goes about with one's looks on the ground, like a man who eyes the bed he is going to lie down in, and longs for. Alice, the crust of the earth seems a barrier between me and my own place. I want to scratch the boardings with my nails and shriek something like this: "Let me get down to you all, there where I belong!" It's a horrible sensation, like a vampire reversed!...'

'Is that why you insisted on having this room in the basement?' she asked breathlessly.

'Yes, I can't bear being upstairs, somehow. Here, with these barred windows and stone-cold floors...I can see the people's feet walking above there in the street...one has some sort of illusion...'

'Oh!' She shivered and her eyes travelled like those of a caged creature round the bare room and fluttered when they rested on the sombre windows imperiously barred. She dropped her gaze to the stone flags that showed beyond the oasis of Turkey carpet on which Arne's chair stood...

Then to the door, the door that she had closed on entering. It had heavy bolts, but they were not drawn against her, though by the look of her eyes it seemed she half imagined they were...

She made a step forward and moved her hands slightly. She looked down on them and what they held...then changed the relative positions of the two objects and held the bottle over the glass...

'Yes, come along!' her husband said. 'Are you going to be all day giving it me?'

With a jerk, she poured the liquid out into a glass and handed it to him. She looked away---towards the door. . .

'Ah, your way of escape!' said he, following her eyes. Then he drank, painstakingly.

The empty bottle fell out of her hands. She wrung them, murmuring--.'Oh, if I had only known!'

'Known what? That I should go near to cursing you for bringing me back?'

He fixed his cold eyes on her, as the liquid passed slowly over his tongue.

'--Or that you would end by taking back the gift you gave?'

THE END